Eva Leaf

I Lost Baby Blue!

Is everyone here?

Red sheep.

Yellow sheep.

Navy Blue lambs.

Orange sheep.

Brown sheep.

Big Black ram.

Grey sheep.

Pink sheep.

...where is Baby Blue?

Lady Green Ewe,
please look too!

Is he by the picnic table?

Or is he by the car?

Is he in the puddle?

Or on the monkey bars?

Wait! A noise!

We found you,
Baby Blue!

Let's celebrate...
with your
favourite cake!

God never gives up when we are lost.
He always finds us.

I LOST BABY BLUE is based on a Jesus story.
You can read it in the Bible, in Luke 15.

Every child deserves the opportunity to step
from their intellect to their heart. I LOST BABY
BLUE presents a sensory way of engaging with
God through colours.

No sheep were bothered in making this book!

Printed in Poland
by Amazon Fulfillment
Poland Sp. z o.o., Wrocław